Ben L. Hughes

Dragon Adventure Series

Book One: A Dragon Named Splinter

Book Two: The Blue Dragon

Book Three: The Dragon Wizard

Book Four: Fire Dragons

Book Five: The Cave of Secrets

Book Six: The Lost Dragons of Fire Island

ISBN-13: 978-1511713207

CreateSpace Independent Publishing Platform

Edited By: Jen Hughes & LJ Cummings

Copyright © 2014 Ben L. Hughes

Revision Date: September 20th, 2015

All Rights Reserved. No part of this book may be reproduced or transmitted in any form or by any means, electronic, mechanical, photocopying, recording, or otherwise, without prior written permission of the Author, except brief portions quoted for review. Any trademarks, service marks, product names or named features are assumed to be the property of their respective owners, and are used only for reference. There is no implied endorsement if one or more of these terms are used.

The characters and events portrayed in this book are fictitious or they are used fictitiously. Any similarities to real persons, living or deceased, is purely coincidental and not intended by the author.

Table of Contents

Chapter 1 4

Chapter 2 11

Chapter 3 14

Chapter 4 27

Chapter 5 40

Chapter 6 48

Chapter 7 57

Chapter 8 65

Chapter 9 83

About the Series 91

Chapter 1

It had been almost a year since Splinter had joined Kevin's family. His parents accepted her as one of their own and they liked how Splinter and Kevin looked after each other. Emalyn's family took in Striker and since they only lived one neighborhood over from Kevin, the dragons and the kids spent a lot of time playing with each other.

Once school let out, Kevin rushed home, and like most days, Splinter was at the door waiting for him.

"Hi Splinter," Kevin said as she flew up into his arms and started nuzzling him with her head. "Okay, that's enough," he laughed.

"I missed you," Splinter replied with a smile.

"I know, I missed you too," Kevin replied. "Did my mom feed you yet?" he asked as he set his backpack down on the floor by the door and then walked over to the kitchen.

"Nope," Splinter said as she tilted her head sideways and blinked her eyes innocently.

"Are you sure?" Kevin questioned.

"It was more like a snack than a meal," Splinter admitted. Then she turned her head all the way upside down, and pointed at her mouth.

"Alright goofball, I'll get you a little more to eat," he chuckled.

A moment later Kevin's mom walked into the kitchen and paused for a moment, "Hey, I already fed her!" she scolded. Splinter folded her ears down and then gulped down the last bits of meat that were in her food bowl.

"She was still hungry," Kevin replied on her behalf.

"You know, I liked it better when I thought dragons were mythical creatures instead of little eating and pooping machines living in my house," Josie exclaimed.

"She's potty trained," Kevin replied in her defense.

"I know…" Josie sighed. She really like Splinter, but it was fun to tease Kevin and it made him appreciate what he had.

A few minutes later, Kevin's dad came walking in and grabbed a beer from the refrigerator. Splinter immediately flew over next to him and then landed on the counter.

"Can I have some?" she asked. Brian instinctively opened up the cabinet and pulled out a small cup for her.

"Dad, if I can't have alcohol, then neither can she!" Kevin insisted.

"You're not 21, but your dragon is," he replied while pouring a little of his beer into the cup for her.

"That's not fair, she's only 21 in dragon years, but we don't know if those are the same as ours. We multiply a dog's age by five," Kevin remarked.

"It's one to one," Splinter said before lapping up the foamy liquid with her tongue.

"See, she's old enough to drink," Brian declared.

"Maybe, but now she'll have beer breath and dragon gas," Kevin said as he held his nose for emphasis. Splinter gave him a dirty look and then flew upstairs after she licked the cup dry.

"I think you insulted her," his dad remarked.

"If I did, then she's probably up on my bed planning some way to get back at me, if she hasn't already," Kevin sighed.

"So, now that you're out of school, I was thinking we should hookup the tent trailer and head over to Wellington Lake this weekend. What do you think?"

"Can we go somewhere new?" Kevin asked.

"I thought you loved that place?" Brian replied.

"I do, but after what happened to Splinter and her brother, I would rather go somewhere new," Kevin admitted.

"Okay," his dad replied. Then he set down his drink so he could search the internet for another campground on his smart phone. While he was fiddling around with that, Splinter came back downstairs and slowly tip-toed over to Brian's unguarded bottle of beer. When Kevin noticed what she was doing, he chuckled under his breath, but didn't say anything. "There's a famous gemstone collecting area down near Buena Vista called Mount Antero. Would you like to go there and try your luck prospecting for gems?" Brian suggested.

"That sounds cool… what's the camp ground like?" Kevin replied, trying not to laugh as Splinter finished off the last of his dad's beer.

"Well, it looks like the campground is near the base of the mountain at about 8,600 feet. From there you take a 4x4 road up to the top of Mount Antero. The gemstone collecting area appears to be on the southwest side of the peak. I think we should bring the ATV, because the map shows Mount Antero is over 14,000 feet high. That's not something we could just climb in one day," Brian exclaimed.

"So what kinds of gemstones are up there?" Kevin asked.

"Aquamarine, Topaz, Smoky Quartz, and a few others according to this website," his dad replied. "It looks like we'll need to bring a shovel and a rock hammer along with us so we can dig for them. It also says you have to be careful not to dig on anyone else's mining claim," his dad added.

"What's a mining claim?" Kevin asked.

"It's a small piece of land that a person has the right to mine for precious metals, gemstones, or other valuable minerals. In the old days, anyone caught on someone else's mining claim could be shot. They were called 'claim jumpers' back then," his dad replied.

"Really?" Kevin asked.

"Yep, a claim is your property. If we found a deposit of gemstones, we could claim it," Brian said optimistically.

"I want to do that," Kevin replied. Then he motioned for Splinter to meet him up in his room.

"Hey! What happened to my beer!" his dad yelled a few minutes later. Kevin and Splinter immediately broke out into laughter. Then when they heard him coming up the stairs, Kevin quickly closed his door and locked it.

"Splinter, I'm going to get you," his dad said jokingly. Splinter stuck her tail out under the door and wiggled it back and forth a couple of times. Then she quickly withdrew it before Brian could grab ahold of it. "That's not funny, I'll get you eventually," Brian promised. Splinter knew better than to try it again, humans were pretty slow, but Brian was faster than most.

Chapter 2

The next day Kevin woke up to the sound of chains rattling along the concrete driveway, followed by a loud metallic clang.

"What's going on out there?" Splinter asked as she flew down from the bunk bed.

"My dad's hooking up the tent trailer to the truck, which means we're going camping," Kevin said in an excited tone.

"Yeah!" Splinter exclaimed.

"Oh, I'm sorry… you don't get to go this time," Kevin replied in a sad, teasing tone.

"What!" Splinter pleaded. "You can't leave your bestest buddy behind!"

"Just kidding," Kevin replied. Splinter immediately poked him in the ear with the tip of her tail until he started to laugh.

"That tickles," he said as he pushed her tail away.

"Oh really?" she remarked innocently.

"You know it does, silly dragon," Kevin replied as he pulled out his backpack and started filling it with clothes for the camping trip.

"Don't forget to bring plenty of dragon treats," Splinter said as she nudged his arm.

"I will," Kevin replied as he zippered his pack closed and then headed downstairs with it.

"Do you need any help?" Splinter asked.

"I suppose you want to help me by taking the bag of treats out to the truck?" Kevin remarked.

"If you insist," Splinter said in an innocent tone.

"Are they safe with you?" Kevin asked.

"Yep, I might have to try one just to make sure they're okay, but that's it," Splinter said in her most sincere tone.

"Alright, I'll get the bag out of the frig." The moment he handed it to her, she flew out to the truck and hid in the backseat. Kevin knew she would eat the whole thing, so it was just a small bag with a few cut up pieces of hotdog in it. The real bag of treats was in the cooler.

"Are you and Splinter ready to go?" his dad asked when he saw Kevin putting his things in the back of the truck.

"We are," Kevin replied. Then he unfolded a small fluffy blanket and set it on the seat next to him.

"How is that?" he asked after Splinter curled up on it.

"Acceptable," she replied with teasing look before changing color to match the fabric. "I don't want anyone to see me when we get out on the highway," she added with a snort.

"They would just think you're a toy dragon," Kevin joked. Splinter immediately reached over and nipped him on the arm.

"Ouch, that hurt! No more reptile treats for you," Kevin scolded.

"There's more?" Splinter asked while affectionately nudging against him.

"If you're good," Kevin remarked as he patted her on the head.

Chapter 3

"How did you sleep?" Brian asked as Kevin emerged from the pop-up mid morning.

"Pretty good," Kevin replied. "Are we heading up the mountain now?"

"Yeah, we have to get up there before the weather turns bad. Fourteeners usually cloud over in the afternoon, and then you have to worry about lightning when you're up near the top," his dad replied.

"What did you say about lightning?" Splinter asked in a worried tone as she flew over next to Kevin.

"Oh right, I forgot about your little mishap with Mother Nature," Brian chuckled.

"I was electrocuted and nearly died!" Splinter insisted.

"Aren't you the one who's always telling us how hard it is to kill a dragon?" Brian asked rhetorically.

"Dad!" Kevin interrupted, "Be nice to my dragon, she's been through a lot."

"Okay, I was just kidding," Brian replied. Then he handed Kevin his helmet and pulled him up onto the ATV.

"What about breakfast?" Kevin asked.

"I put a bunch of snacks in my backpack… and yes, there are dragon treats in there too," he added with a smile.

"Is mom coming with us?" Kevin asked.

"No, she's going to stay down here and relax. I'm not sure digging through dirt and rocks is her idea of a good time," Brian remarked.

"Okay," Kevin replied. Then he set Splinter on his lap once he was ready to go.

The trail wound its way up through the trees for the first several miles. As they passed by a waterfall Kevin's dad pulled over and took a couple of pictures of it.

"That's pretty," Splinter remarked before they started back up the trail.

When they reached the tree line at 11,000 feet, Kevin's dad pulled off of the trail so he could take a few more pictures and stretch his legs.

"That's Mount Antero," he said pointing directly ahead of them. Kevin's eyes followed the steep trail as it dotted its way up along the side of the mountain.

"We're going up that?" he asked in a disbelieving tone.

"Yep," his dad replied, suppressing any doubts that the ATV might not make it all the way to the summit.

Little by little they forged on. The ATV started to sputter after they passed by a hand carved wooden sign that read, '13,000 feet' on it. The air was noticeably thinner and cooler, so Kevin zipped up his jacket and then looked down at Splinter.

"Are you warm enough?" he asked as he placed his hand on her side.

"I'm fine," she replied, amused by the fact that humans needed so many layers of clothing to be comfortable.

"Let's stop here and look around," Brian suggested when they reached a large flat area known as the south saddle. It was a mile long expanse that bridged the summit of Mount Antero with its slightly smaller neighbor, Mount White.

"So what do the gemstones look like?" Kevin asked as he climbed off the ATV.

"Blue aquamarines, yellow topaz, and smoky quartz," his dad answered. "The best gemstones are found in pockets and pegmatite veins. The other thing to keep an eye out for are gemstones that have weathered out of their veins, and might be mixed in with the loose rocks on the surface. That's probably our best bet for finding something today," Brian admitted.

"Okay," Kevin replied as he picked up a trowel and headed diagonally along the base of Mount Antero's summit. Splinter followed after him while Kevin's dad walked over to examine an interesting outcropping of rocks just above them.

"Find anything yet?" Brian called out after they had been searching for a while.

"I found one rock with a small light blue crystal on it," Kevin replied. Then he handed the specimen to Splinter, who flew it over to his dad.

"It looks like an aquamarine to me," Brian remarked after looking it over for a minute. "Not gem quality, but it's still a nice sample," he added.

Kevin immediately started to dig in the spot where he had found the aquamarine. After excavating a sizeable hole without finding anything else, he moved further up the hill. From time to time Splinter would bring a rock over for Kevin to look at, but none of them appeared to be gemstones.

"I'm not having much luck," Kevin said as he looked over at his dad.

"It's been picked over pretty good. Sorry, I didn't know," his dad said in a disappointed tone.

"I think a raindrop just hit me," Kevin announced.

"Yeah, we better pack it up," his dad said after looking up at the swirling clouds.

"I wish we would have found something better," Kevin remarked as he walked back to the ATV.

"I know, next time we'll have to bring some dynamite with us," his dad said with a smile. Kevin laughed and then climbed up on the ATV. Splinter immediately flew into his lap when she heard a distant rumble of thunder.

"Are you ready to go?" Brian asked.

"I am," Kevin replied. Splinter nodded and then lowered her head down as if that would protect her from the weather.

Once they reached the tree line, Kevin tugged on his dad's jacket, signaling he wanted him to stop.

"What is it?" Brian asked as he pulled off of the trail.

"I need to use the bathroom," Kevin replied as he eyed a group of small windblown trees a few paces away. His dad nodded and then turned off the ATV.

Kevin quickly ran behind the trees and didn't reappear.

"Kevin?" his dad yelled out when he thought enough time had passed.

"Do you want me to fly over and see what's keeping him?" Splinter offered.

"Where is he?" Brian asked with a concerned look on his face when Splinter returned without him.

"Don't worry, he's not hurt, but he fell through some rotten boards that were covering the entrance to a mine," Splinter reported. Brian immediately jumped off the ATV and ran over behind the trees.

"Are you okay?" he asked as he peered down into the dark hole where his son had fallen.

"I'm fine!" Kevin yelled back, sounding a bit embarrassed.

"Thank goodness," his dad replied. I have a roll of para-cord back at the ATV, just stay where you are and I'll be right back to get you out!"

"Okay dad," Kevin replied.

A few minutes later Brian returned with a flashlight and a roll of para-cord. After he unraveled the cord, he lowered it and the flashlight into the hole so Kevin could reach it.

"Just wrap the para-cord around your waist and then tie it tight... use more than one knot," his dad instructed.

"Where are you going?" Brian asked in an anxious voice when Kevin stepped out of his sight for a moment.

"Nowhere, I'm just finishing up the knot," Kevin replied after zipping his jacket closed.

"You will have to use your feet to climb up as I pull on the para-cord, but don't worry, I won't let you fall," his dad promised.

"Alright, I'm ready," Kevin replied. His dad slowly backed away from the edge, and then started pulling him up. When he reached the top, Brian grabbed his hand and lifted him the rest of the way out.

"Are you sure you're not hurt?" Brian asked as he looked him over.

"I'm fine," Kevin replied as he brushed the dirt off his pants. Splinter rushed over and licked him on the cheek until he personally reassured her that he was okay.

"Was it scary down there," Splinter asked.

"A little, but I think I found something valuable while I was down there," Kevin said as he reached into his jacket and pulled out an antique looking silver box.

"What is that?" Splinter asked as her eyes lit up with excitement.

"I don't know," Kevin replied as he handed it to his dad so he could take a closer look at it.

"This is really old," Brian remarked as he brushed some of the dirt and ice off the top of it.

"How old?" Kevin asked.

"I don't know, but the writing looks Celtic and I think the box is made of silver," his dad said as he examined it more closely.

"Is that why it feels so heavy?" Kevin asked.

"No, there's something in it," Brian replied.

"Should we open it up so we can see what's inside?" Kevin suggested, as he hoped it would be filled with treasure.

"I think it's locked," his dad replied after gently prying on the lid. Then he carefully turned it on its side and saw a small keyhole on the front. "Maybe if we had something small and hook shaped we could release the locking mechanism."

"What about this?" Splinter offered as she held out her tail.

"Okay," Brian replied. Then he held the box steady while Splinter twisted and turned her tail several times.

After a couple of attempts, the box made a clicking sound, and the lid sprung open.

"Are those eggs?" Kevin asked with an air of disappointment as he peered into the box.

"I think so," his dad replied, unsure as to what type of eggs they were.

"Those are dragon eggs!" Splinter said with a look of shock on her face.

"Are you kidding me?" Kevin said in disbelief.

"No, those are definitely dragon eggs," Splinter insisted.

"Pigmy Dragon eggs?" Kevin questioned.

"No, they're too big for that," Splinter replied as she picked one up to look at it. "Oh my gosh!" she gasped when the sunlight illuminated the egg.

"What's wrong?" Kevin asked.

"The dragon inside this egg is still alive!" Splinter announced in disbelief. Then she gently set the egg back into the box and carefully inspected the other two. "These are alive as well!"

"Can they still hatch?" Kevin inquired.

"If they warm up, I don't see why not," Splinter replied.

"How can that be? They're so old," Brian questioned.

"Well, I know Pigmy Dragon eggs have been know to hatch many years after being laid if they were kept cold," Splinter revealed.

"Okay, but this box looks like it might be hundreds of years old," Brian remarked. "Are you sure the eggs are still good?"

"They look fine to me, but we would need to show them to Luxor to know for sure," Splinter replied as she glanced at them.

"Who's Luxor?" Kevin asked.

"Um… he's the one you call the blue dragon," Splinter said in a hesitant tone.

"Do we dare go back there?" Kevin exclaimed.

"I don't think you realize the significance of these eggs. The simple fact that I don't recognize them means they belong to some rare or unknown species of dragon. These eggs might be the last of their kind in the world."

"Could they be Water Dragon eggs?" Kevin suggested.

"They are the correct size and shape, but Water Dragon eggs are pearlescent, and as you can see these are very dark."

"Is that because they are so old?" Kevin asked.

"I don't think so, but that is why I think I need to consult with Luxor. His knowledge of dragon history dates back over a thousand years. If anyone knows what kind of eggs these are, it will be him," Splinter insisted.

"You two can decide what to do with the eggs later," Brian interjected. "I think we should probably head back now so your mom doesn't start to worry about us... and one more thing, when we get back to the camp, let me do the talking. I don't want the tunnel incident to be dramatized," Brian added as he looked over at Kevin.

"Dad, I don't do that," Kevin replied, but his father just rolled his eyes and then headed back over to the ATV without responding.

Once everyone was seated, he started it up, and they continued down the trail.

Chapter 4

On the way back from camping at Mount Antero, Kevin's dad stopped in Bailey to get gas and then turned down the road leading to Wellington Lake.

"You're such a marshmallow," Josie said as she looked over at Brian while shaking her head from side to side.

"What?" Brian replied. "Splinter and Kevin need to solve the mystery of the dragon eggs."

"I think you and your son have watched too many Scooby-Doo episodes."

"Perhaps, but in all seriousness, Splinter seems to think the dragons inside the eggs are still alive. There is no harm in having them checked out, especially if they're rare," Brian suggested.

"I agree," Josie said as she opened the lid to take another look at the eggs. "It does seem like someone went to a lot of trouble to keep these safe," she added after seeing how each egg fit perfectly inside the satin lined box.

"Yeah, and I think the box is made of real silver," Brian remarked.

"The design looks Celtic," Josie replied.

"I thought so too."

"I wonder who it belonged to, and why they left it in an abandoned mine?" Josie asked as she gently set it back down.

"It's hard to say," Brian responded as they continued down the gravel road towards Wellington Lake.

"So, what's the plan when we get there?" Kevin asked as he looked over at Splinter.

"I will fly up to the top of Castle Mountain and see if I can find Luxor. If I am successful, then I will ask him to come down with me and examine the eggs," Splinter answered.

"I don't like that plan," Kevin confessed. "What if Luxor decides to detain you because you are still living with humans?"

"I don't think that will happen, he knew we were going to stay with you."

"You are still breaking the law, and you will be on your own up there," Kevin said in a worried tone.

"Once I describe the eggs to him, I am confident he will want to see them. Like I said before, I believe they are extremely rare," Splinter insisted.

"Alright, but I'm coming to rescue you if don't come back in a reasonable amount of time," Kevin promised.

"There is one more thing," Splinter added. "If I am successful in getting Luxor to come back with me, it would be best if your parents weren't around. Luxor knows you, but I don't believe he will help us if he sees your parents nearby," Splinter said as diplomatically as she could.

"I heard that," Brian interrupted as he pulled into the campground.

"Dad, stop snooping," Kevin said with a frown.

"Alright, your mom and I can take a walk around the lake while you two meet with Luxor if you like?" Brian offered.

"Yes please," Kevin replied.

After his dad drove around to the back side of the lake, he parked the truck and then left with Josie.

Once they were out of sight, Kevin got out of the truck with Splinter.

"I'll be back as soon as I can," Splinter said as she gave Kevin a reassuring look. Then she flew off towards Castle Mountain while he sat at a picnic table waiting for her return.

Every minute that Splinter was gone Kevin's mind kept playing all the worst-case scenarios it could come up with. He hated the idea that she was up there by herself, and wished he had never agreed to it. After what seemed like an eternity of waiting, Splinter landed on the picnic table next to him and uncloaked after she saw that there was no one else around.

"You're back!" Kevin said with a sigh of relief. "How did it go?"

"Good," Splinter replied as Luxor uncloaked on the table next to her.

"So let's see those eggs," he grumbled. Kevin nodded and then went inside the truck to retrieve the box. A moment later he set the box on the table and opened it up.

"It can't be..." Luxor exclaimed as he looked on in amazement.

"Do you know what kind of dragon eggs they are?" Splinter asked.

"They're Fire Dragon eggs!" Luxor replied as he lifted one up to examine it more closely, "and they're still alive!"

"I told you," Splinter remarked.

"Where did you find them?" Luxor asked as he looked over at Splinter.

"Kevin found them," she answered.

"You are an extraordinary boy," Luxor said as he eyed Kevin suspiciously. "Not only are you the first human to have befriended a dragon in a millennium, but now you've discovered Fire Dragon eggs. A species that we all thought to be extinct... my goodness, what forces are at work in you young man?"

Kevin didn't reply, unsure of what to make of Luxor's assessment of him.

"Kevin found the eggs in an abandoned mine up on Mount Antero," Splinter remarked.

"How high up were they?" Luxor asked.

"It was right at the edge of the tree line," Splinter replied.

"How fortunate... whoever put them there must have known that freezing temperatures would prevent them from hatching and also keep them preserved," Luxor stated as he inspected the box.

"What do you make of it?" Kevin asked, when he realized Luxor was admiring it.

"It's from the medieval period," he replied. "Made by a master silversmith who designed it specifically for these eggs," he added.

"So, a human wanted to preserve them?" Kevin asked in a cautious tone.

"It would appear so," Luxor admitted.

"What should I do with the eggs?" Kevin asked.

"Well they're going to hatch now that they have warmed up," Luxor replied.

"You should take them," Kevin suggested.

"Oh no, Fire Dragons can't camouflage themselves like we can. They would be seen by the humans that come here, and then we would be forced to move!" Luxor exclaimed with a disapproving snort.

"I don't understand. If these are so rare, you need to take them and protect them," Kevin insisted.

"No, Castle Mountain is our sacred home." Luxor said without elaborating further. Kevin could tell that there was a lot more to this story than Luxor was saying, but he didn't want to push the issue.

"I don't think my parents are going to let me keep three more dragons at my house."

"Do you have any other friends that you can trust to take care of them, someone who can keep their existence, and ours, a secret?" Luxor suggested.

"What about your law about keeping hidden and not interacting with humans?" Kevin questioned.

"The law was enacted to protect the surviving species of dragons, but what you have discovered is outside of the law. You must find them a home away from this place," Luxor insisted.

"Okay, I'll do that, but I need to know more about them," Kevin remarked.

"I will tell you what I know," Luxor agreed.

"How big are they going to get?"

"About twenty feet long when they're full grown… but they only need to be looked after until they are able to survive on their own," Luxor replied.

"So, exactly how old do they need to be before that happens?" Kevin asked hesitantly.

"Three months should be enough," Luxor answered.

"That might work, but what about the whole breathing fire thing?" Kevin asked.

"They can't breathe fire until they reach maturity. I don't know at what age that will happen for them, but I am sure it's not for many months," Luxor asserted.

"I think my friend David might be willing to take care of them. His family has a large unfinished basement that could work as a dragon nursery depending on what else they might need," Kevin hinted.

"All they need is water, meat, and someone to teach them dragon etiquette. Splinter and her brother could help your friend with that part," Luxor suggested as he looked over at Splinter.

"My brother and I would be happy to help," Splinter replied. "We can even assist David in finding a suitable place to let the dragons go, when that time comes."

"It sounds like you have the problem solved," Luxor remarked.

"Yeah, I'll see if my friend is willing to raise the dragons. To be honest, I think he will be excited about the prospect of having them," Kevin revealed.

"Why would a human be excited about taking care of a dragon?" Luxor asked as he looked over at Splinter.

"After spending a year living with Kevin, I can tell you a lot has changed since the old days. Humans have children's books about us and cartoons where we live amongst them and help them," Splinter explained.

"Yeah, but that's just fairytale kid's stuff," Luxor alleged. "In the real world humans would imprison us in zoos, scientists would dissect us, and those who fear us would have us exterminated like some pest."

"I don't think that's true anymore," Splinter contended. "From what I have seen, even the adults have changed their view of us. Dragons are actually portrayed as majestic and powerful creatures in their lore. Some of Kevin's ancestors are from Wales, and Draig Goch is depicted on their national flag. If that's not enough, Kevin's father has a Fire Dragon tattooed on his arm and his mom wears a golden dragon pendant around her neck. I could cite a dozen more examples if you like," Splinter added.

Luxor looked down for a moment as he thought about what Splinter had said. Then he turned to Kevin and asked, "If you and your family honor dragons, and your ancestors are from Wales, then you might be a descendant of the Dragon Wizard."

"I doubt that," Kevin scoffed, not really sure who or what Luxor was referring to.

"Perhaps not," Luxor snorted as he camouflaged himself and then flew off.

"What's a dragon wizard?" Kevin asked Splinter after Luxor was gone.

"When humans discovered gold in southern Wales, they captured a large and powerful Fire Dragon named Draig Goch. Then they forced him to work at gold mine near the Cothi River. At the mine, there was a young slave woman whose job it was to feed him and clean his cage each day. Over time, the two became friends and learned to trust each other.

One day the slave woman revealed that she was pregnant, and since she was a slave, her child would be forced into servitude or killed since she could not care for it. Rather than see her offspring taken from her, she and Draig formed a pact. Once the child was born, she would set Draig free, and he would protect the child and see that he was taken care of.

Their plan apparently worked, and after the woman gave birth to a little boy, Draig took the child and cared for him. Since Draig knew that the child would need to learn about life from other humans in order to fit into their society, he bartered with a local sheepherder and they took him in and raised him as their own.

As the boy grew, it was said that he had the power to heal sick or injured animals. When the war between dragons and humans spread, he used his gift to save the dragons that needed his help. He wasn't able to stop the war, but in a time when dragons were demonized, he was one of the few humans that fought to protect them. No one ever knew what became of the boy who could heal dragons, but the tale of his deeds has been handed down for generations. In fact, he is known by dragons everywhere as the Dragon Wizard.

"What an incredible story. Do you believe it's true?" Kevin asked.

"It was a long time ago," Splinter replied.

"I never knew that the dragon on the Welsh flag was Draig Goch. I wonder why my ancestors chose a dragon for their flag when they fought against them in the middle ages?"

"Maybe your ancestors did not participate in that fight, or maybe they fought for the other side," Splinter hinted.

"I guess we'll never know," Kevin said as he pulled the radio out of his pocket and depressed the transmit button. "Dad, Splinter and I are ready to go."

"Okay, we're on our way back," his dad replied.

Chapter 5

When Kevin got back home the first thing he did was call Emalyn and tell her about the discovery of the Fire Dragon eggs.

"That's so amazing," Emalyn replied when he finished the lengthy story.

"What do you think is the best way to tell David about the dragons?" Kevin asked.

"I don't know… maybe I could come over with Striker and together we can let him in on our little secret," Emalyn suggested.

"That's a good idea. If he sees we both have dragons, then hopefully he will want them too," Kevin replied.

"I am sure he will, you know how excited he gets over baby animals," Emalyn remarked.

"Yeah, let me give him a call and see if he is free, but either way, you and Striker might as well come over. I know Splinter has been wanting to play with her brother," Kevin suggested.

"Sure, we'll be there in a little bit," Emalyn replied.

"Okay, I'll see you then." After Kevin got off the phone with Emalyn he immediately called David.

"Hello?" David replied.

"Hey, it's me," Kevin said in a familiar tone.

"What's going on?" David questioned as if sensing Kevin was up to something.

"Can you come over? Emalyn and I have something to show you," Kevin remarked.

"Is everything okay?" David asked suspiciously.

"Yeah, I just can't tell you over the phone, it's more of a show, than a tell," Kevin insisted.

"Alright, I'll be over as soon as I can."

A few minutes later the doorbell rang and Kevin rushed downstairs to see who it was.

"Hi Emalyn, hi Striker," Kevin said as he let them inside.

"Is David coming over?" Emalyn asked after noticing he wasn't there.

"Yeah, he's on his way," Kevin replied.

"How are the eggs doing?" Striker asked.

"They look the same to me, but Splinter said they are really close to hatching," Kevin replied.

"Where is my little sister?" Striker asked.

"She's upstairs hiding from you," Kevin whispered. Striker immediately flew off in search of her. When he reached the top of the stairs and started to turn the corner, Splinter pounced on him. Then they rolled around on the carpet in a dragon ball laughing at each other, before heading into Kevin's bedroom.

"Don't destroy my room," Kevin reminded them, thinking back to the last time when Striker had come over. On that visit, Striker had pulled all the blankets off of his bed and made forts out of them.

"Here comes David," Emalyn announced after peeking through the blinds on the front window.

"Oh, thanks, I'll let him in," Kevin replied. Then as David ran up to the door, Kevin opened it for him.

"So, what's going on?" David asked.

"Why don't you follow Emalyn and I up to my room, the surprise is in there," Kevin hinted.

"Okay," David replied, half expecting it to be some new computer game or cool toy.

As Kevin slowly pushed the door open, David stood there speechless for several minutes as he watched the dragons playing with each other.

"Are those real?" David asked in disbelief.

"Yep, Emalyn and I have pet dragons. The bright green one is Splinter and the darker green one is her brother Striker," Kevin said proudly.

"Oh my gosh, they're so cute. Are they baby dragons?" he yelled with excitement. Splinter immediately stopped chasing her brother and looked over at David. Then she said, "We're not baby dragons, we're Pigmy Dragons!"

"They can talk!" David yelled out in a burst of uncontrollable excitement.

"Yes they can," Kevin calmly replied.

"Where did you get them?"

"Emalyn and I rescued them when we went camping awhile back… it's kind of a long story, so I'll tell that part later. The real reason I wanted you to come over is because Emalyn and I need your help. We have three dragon eggs that are going to hatch soon and we don't have anyone to take care of them…"

"I'll do it!" David blurted out.

"Okay, but these eggs aren't Pigmy Dragons eggs, they're from a Fire Dragon. The last ones in existence," Kevin added with emphasis.

"Okay, so what do I need to do?" David asked.

"Would your parents let you use your basement as a dragon nursery?"

"Yeah, nobody uses it," David replied.

"Good, because unlike Pigmy Dragons, these dragons are going to get big. They are also going to be able to breathe fire once they mature, so you won't be able to keep them as pets," Kevin insisted.

"Okay. So, how long will I need to care for them?" David asked.

"Well, there haven't been any Fire Dragons around since medieval times, so it's a bit of a guess… but they should be able to survive on their own after about three months," Kevin replied.

"Okay, so after they hatch what do I feed them?" David asked as he looked down at Splinter and Striker who were still playing with each other.

"The closest thing we have to dragon milk is probably baby formula," Kevin remarked as he looked at Splinter to see if she thought that would work.

"That's close enough," Splinter responded, as she held her brother down long enough to answer the question. "They can have meat as soon as their teeth come in," she added.

"Cooked or raw?" David asked.

"Either," Splinter answered. "Dragons aren't picky."

"No kidding," Kevin said with a smirk. Splinter snorted at him, and then started clowning around with her brother again.

"Is there anything else I need to know?" David asked as he looked over at Kevin.

"I think that's it, but all of us will help you as much as we can," Kevin replied.

"I'm surprised you and Emalyn aren't keeping the eggs and raising the baby dragons yourselves," David remarked.

"Neither of us have a place to set up a dragon nursery… and you're the only friend that I can trust to keep this secret," Kevin admitted.

"What do I tell my parents about the eggs?" David asked.

"You're going to have to tell them the truth," Kevin suggested.

"Do you think they are going to believe me when I show them the eggs and say they are from a dragon?" David scoffed.

"Maybe not… I'll have my mom tell your mom about the dragons. Then they will know that you are telling the truth about the eggs," Kevin suggested.

"That's a good idea," David replied as he reached down to touch one of the dragons. When Striker saw what he was doing, he pushed Splinter out of the way so he could get petted instead of her.

"Hey!" she exclaimed. Then she bit her brother on the tail playfully.

Chapter 6

The next morning Kevin saw David's mom Toni pull into their driveway from his bedroom window.

"Hey mom, your friend Toni is here," Kevin called out from his room.

"Okay," Josie replied as she went down to let her friend in.

"Hi Josie, I'm sorry to bother you, but David insisted that I come over right away," Toni sighed.

"Oh good, I was going to invite you over so we could talk about some things," Josie replied.

"I know all about your son's pet dragon, David won't stop talking it," Toni said in total disbelief.

"You realized that he is telling the truth?" Josie asked.

"Oh, you're such a good mom, always supporting your son's creativity. I'm just not sure he should be telling David that dragons are real. Now, he's convinced that he saw one," Toni laughed.

"David is telling the truth," Josie replied.

"I think kids should have vivid imaginations... wait, did you just say he's telling the truth?" Toni questioned.

"Yes, Kevin does have a real pet dragon," Josie replied. "I'll have him bring her down so you can see for yourself... but you might want to sit down for this."

"Okay," Toni said with a cautious laugh, half expecting Kevin to come down with a stuffed animal in his hands.

"Her name is Splinter," Kevin said as he walked over to Toni so she could see the dragon. Toni sat there speechless, as Splinter curled up in Kevin's arms and yawned.

Once Toni recovered from the initial shock of seeing a real dragon, Josie explained the story of how Kevin and Emalyn had saved her. Then she told Toni about the Fire Dragon eggs and how they needed someone to raise them.

"Well, I guess I owe my son an apology," Toni said after Kevin took Splinter back to his room.

"Are you going to let David take care of the dragon eggs?" Josie asked.

"I have to now, it's the only way he will ever forgive me for not believing him," Toni admitted.

"You'll have to keep all of this a secret," Josie remarked.

"Oh, I definitely will," Toni replied. "If word of this got out, my house would be turned into a circus. You know how the media loves to turn everything into a freak show."

"Yeah, I don't believe half of what they say anymore," Josie added.

"Well, I better get back home, David is probably wearing out the carpet by the front door," Toni remarked.

"Thanks for stopping by, I'll let Kevin know your leaving so he can give you the eggs," Josie said as she called up the stairs for him.

A few moments later, Kevin can down with the silver box tightly clutched in both hands.

"They're the last of their kind," Kevin said in a protective voice.

"I'll make sure that David takes good care of them," Toni replied.

"Thank you for helping us," Kevin said with a smile.

"You're welcome," she replied before heading out the door.

Once Toni was gone, Kevin thanked his mom for talking to her, and then returned to his room.

Later that day, Kevin received a text from David that the first egg had a small crack in the shell and he thought it might be starting to hatch.

"I'll be right over," he texted back. Then he ran out to the garden looking for his mom.

"What's up?" she asked as he came running over to her.

"David said the first egg is starting to hatch… can Splinter and I go over and see it."

"Sure, just be back before dinner," she replied.

"Thanks mom," Kevin said as he rushed off to get Splinter.

"What's going on?" Splinter asked when he woke her up from her afternoon nap.

"One of the eggs is starting to hatch," Kevin replied in an excited tone.

"Okay, tuck me in a blanket and let's go." Splinter could have camouflaged herself and flown over to David's house first, but she didn't want Kevin to feel left out.

"Has the egg hatched yet?" Kevin asked the moment David opened the door to let them in.

"No, but the other two eggs have some cracks in them now," David said with a look of excitement and concern.

"Does Emalyn know what's going on?" Kevin asked as he and Splinter followed David into the basement.

"Yeah, she's already here," David replied.

"Hi Kevin, hi Splinter," Emalyn said in a friendly voice.

"Hi, you sure got here fast," Kevin remarked.

"I rode my bike," she replied. Everyone suddenly went silent when one of the eggs made a cracking sound. An instant later a small dark red baby dragon head popped out through the shell and looked around the room at them. The basement immediately filled with 'ooh's' and 'awes' as the little creature freed itself from the egg.

"See if the dragon is hungry," David said to Emalyn who was standing closest to the bottle of formula.

"Okay," she replied, seemingly mesmerized by the little fellow. "He likes it," she said enthusiastically after the dragon started to drink from it.

"Is it a boy or a girl?" Kevin asked as he looked over at Splinter.

"It's a boy," Splinter replied. "Male dragons are always much darker in color than the females. That's why I'm a beautiful shimmering green and my brother looks like a ball of dried mud," she teased.

"Hey!" Striker remarked. "What did I do?" Just then, a second egg popped open, revealing a dark gray dragon with black scales running down his spine.

"Another boy," Splinter exclaimed.

"I'll feed this one," David said as he reached across the table for a bottle of formula.

The dragon sniffed the formula for a moment and then started to drink it. David smiled when the little dragon paused to burp, before gulping more of it down.

A moment later the third egg started to crack open and then went silent.

"Should we help the dragon break out?" Emalyn asked with a concerned look on her face.

"Not yet, we don't want to accidently hurt the dragon," Splinter advised.

After a few moments of anxiously waiting, a little green nose poked through the shell and took several deep breaths.

"You can do it," Emalyn said in an encouraging tone. Then the dragon pushed with all its might and the egg split down the middle to reveal a light green dragon with golden tipped scales.

Splinter gasped with excitement, "it's a girl...and in the rarest of all colors... gilded."

Kevin retrieved the third bottle of formula from the edge of the table and held it close to the dragon's little nose. The dragon sniffed the end of the bottle and then glanced over at her brothers who were gulping theirs down like two pigs. After a few more sniffs of the mysterious liquid, she finally decided to try it.

"Oh, she likes it," Kevin remarked as he steadied the bottle for her. After she finished, she curled up next to her brothers and fell asleep.

"They're so cute," Emalyn said as she patted Striker on the head.

"I know," David acknowledged. "I wish I could keep them forever."

"You might change your mind when they're twenty feet long and setting your house on fire," Striker joked.

"Well, I better head back home," Emalyn announced before taking one last look at the baby dragons.

"Me too," Kevin added with a sigh as he followed her up the stairs.

"If you have any questions, contact me or my brother," Splinter added as she flew up after Kevin.

"I will," David replied. Then he pulled up a chair and turned down the lights so the little dragons could rest.

Chapter 7

Emalyn and Kevin went over to David's house every chance they had. They knew that when the summer ended, the dragons would have to be set free. Kevin knew it was going to be hardest on David, so he worked out a plan with Splinter that he thought might help. Then he and Splinter went over to his house after lunch so they could talk to him about it.

After ringing the doorbell a couple of times, David came to the door and let them in.

"Sorry about that, I was out back with Charlie. He needed a potty break," David remarked.

"How is he adjusting to the dragons?" Kevin asked.

"I don't how well dogs and dragons mix, so I keep Charlie out of the basement," David replied as he looked over at Splinter.

"They should be fine," Splinter remarked.

"Did you want to see the dragons?" David asked.

"Yeah, but Splinter had a question for you," Kevin replied.

"Okay, what's up?" he asked.

"I know it's several moths away, but once the Fire Dragons are gone I could come spend some time with you?" Splinter offered.

"That's really nice of you, but I have known from the beginning that they would not be pets," David admitted.

"Alright, but if you start to go through dragon withdrawal, I'm here to help… and if you have any left over dragon treats, I would be happy to dispose of those for you," Splinter added.

"It's funny how you work dragon treats into every situation," David laughed. Splinter winked her eyes at him and then flew off.

"Speaking of dragons, how are the little ones doing?" Kevin asked.

"They are growing like crazy. The boys like to play rough with their sister, but even though she is a little smaller than them, she's definitely the boss."

"Really? They don't hurt each other when they play?" Kevin asked.

"No, apparently their scales are harder than they look," David remarked as he opened the door to the basement.

"I think we should name them now that they are developing their own unique personalities," Kevin suggested.

"No sappy human names!" Splinter interjected as she flew down the stairs after them.

"What about Buzz Lightyear?" David said jokingly. Splinter immediately swooped down and bit him on the butt before he could reach the bottom.

"Ouch!" he yelled out, rubbing the spot with his hand.

"That was nothing warm-blood, suggest another silly name and see what happens," she said while bearing her teeth at him.

"No sense of humor in that dragon," David remarked under his breath.

"What about naming the dark red one Draig in honor of the great dragon Draig Goch from long ago?" Kevin suggested.

"That would be acceptable," Splinter acknowledged.

"Can we call the other boy dragon Ironstone, on account of his coloration?" David asked as he moved a little further back from where Splinter had landed.

"Perhaps you should call Emalyn so she can name the girl dragon," Splinter suggested.

"Okay," David replied. After a short conversation with her over the phone, David said, "Esmeralda?"

"Esmeralda y Oro," Splinter muttered to herself before responding. "Emerald and gold, just like her rare color. That will do nicely. I think that now that they are named, we should start thinking about where we can set them free," Splinter suggested.

"What kind of habitat do they need for survival?" David asked.

"Fire Dragons used to live along the Mediterranean and up into northern Europe based on what Luxor told us. The most important thing to remember is that Fire Dragons can't camouflage themselves, so they are going to need an area where humans rarely go. Caves would be a plus, and there has to be an abundance of small to medium sized animals or fish for them to feed on," Splinter added.

"The southwest is the only area I know of that is remote enough for them to go unnoticed," David replied.

"What about somewhere near Lake Powell?" Kevin suggested, "There's an abundance of large fish in the lake, but I can't remember if there are any caves in the area."

"Let me go check," David said as he ran upstairs to find his laptop. While they waited for David to return, Kevin and Splinter started playing with the young dragons.

"They're almost as big as you are," Kevin noted as he picked one up to tickle it on the stomach.

"Yeah, I think they have reached their maximum cuteness," Splinter replied.

"I have some good news," David yelled out as he came running down the stairs with his laptop

"What did you find?" Kevin asked.

"Lake Powell might be the perfect spot. The lake has over 2000 miles of shoreline, so finding a secluded area shouldn't be that hard. Unfortunately, the only caves I could find are well known and visited by people. There are some abandoned uranium mines on the far side of the lake, but I'm not sure if dragons could live in those or not," David remarked.

"It doesn't matter if it's a cave or an old mine," Splinter replied. "Dragons are perfectly at home in either.

"Won't the radioactivity from the uranium hurt them?" David asked.

"No, our scales not only protect us from getting sunburns, but they block out other forms of radiation as well."

"I like the idea of abandoned mines. People generally avoid them, and I bet uranium mines would be especially unpopular," Kevin remarked.

"Yeah, we just have to figure how to get them there," David added.

"We still have lots of time to figure that out," Kevin said as he pulled out his phone to see what time it was.

"Do you have to go?' David asked.

"Yeah, we should head back home. It's almost dinner time, and you know how dragons get when they miss a meal," Kevin joked. Splinter squinted her eyes at him and then flew up the stairs.

"Alright, I'll see you later," David replied. Then he picked up a rubber dog toy, and started playing tug-a-war with the Fire Dragons.

"Your friend David seems to be getting pretty attached to the little ones," Splinter mentioned while they were walking back home.

"I know, it's going to be hard for him to let them go, even though he won't admit it," Kevin sighed.

"They are going to get really big and unruly if he waits too long," Splinter added.

"I wouldn't worry about that, David wants what's best for the dragons, and if that means letting them go, then he will," Kevin insisted.

Chapter 8

As the months passed by, the dragons continued to grow and become more independent. Esmeralda held her position as the most dominate of the three, and it was clear that she was a natural leader. Draig was the largest of the three dragons, measuring four feet long head to tail. His disposition was calm and respectful, while also being confident. David really liked his personality and he knew it would be hard to see him go. Ironstone was the most precocious of the three, and seemed to find new ways to get into trouble.

"Breakfast time," David announced as came down the stairs with their food bowls. When he reached the last step, Ironstone sneak-attacked him and he dropped their food bowls on the floor. Ironstone quickly ate up the spilled food and then hid behind the storage boxes stacked in the corner.

"Ironstone!" David yelled in a parental tone. "Now I have to go back upstairs and get more food for your siblings."

"Can you get me some more while you're up there?" he said as he peeked out from his hiding place.

"Ugh!" David sighed. "All you do is eat and poop!"

"Is he really mad at me?" Ironstone asked when David left the room.

"I don't know," Draig replied, sounding a bit unsure if he really was or not. Ironstone huffed, and then went over to the basement window and stared out of it. "I'm leaving," he said as he unlatched the window with his tail and slid it open.

"Get back in here!" Draig yelled, but before he could stop him, Ironstone jumped out.

"Let him go," Esmeralda said in a disappointed tone. "He'll be back when his stomach starts to grumble."

"I don't think so," Draig replied. "He's been sneaking out at night and hunting in the field behind David's house."

"Oh no, that fool probably thinks he can survive on his own," Esmeralda remarked in a nervous tone.

"I guess I should have mentioned it before now, but I thought he just needed some freedom from the basement," Draig admitted.

"If he gets caught we're all going to be in big trouble… I think we better go get him!" Esmeralda said as she jumped out the window.

"Should I tell David what Ironstone did before we go?" Draig asked.

"No, let's try and get him back before anyone sees him," Esmeralda replied.

"Alright," Draig said as he followed out. He stayed close behind her, ducking behind bushes and large clumps of grass as they tracked Ironstone's footprints across the dusty field.

"There he is," Esmeralda whispered as she pointed towards the far edge of the abandoned pasture. They could clearly see Ironstone was perched over a prairie dog hole next to the road that led into David's neighborhood.

"That idiot is going to be seen for sure," Draig snorted as they crept towards him. When they were just within yelling distance, three cars suddenly turned onto the road leading into the subdivision. Draig and Esmeralda froze and then looked on nervously as the cars approached. The first vehicle sped past Ironstone, seemingly unaware of the large gray dragon standing out in the field. The second car also passed by without noticing him. The third car passed Ironstone, and when Esmeralda was about to stand up and call for him, it suddenly stopped, and then started backing up.

"Run!" Esmeralda yelled out. Ironstone immediately looked in their direction, and then saw the car had veered off the road and was heading straight towards him.

"Run! They're going to catch you!" Draig yelled out as loud as he could. Ironstone bolted in their direction and then all three of them ran across the field towards David's house. The car chased after them, getting closer with each passing minute.

"Faster, he's gaining on us!" Draig yelled. The car's engine roared behind them, and then suddenly stopped. When Draig looked back, he could see the driver waving his arms in frustration when his car couldn't get over the drainage ditch.

"What were you thinking?" Esmeralda scolded once they all got back inside the basement.

"I don't know..." Ironstone replied as he sulked in the corner.

"You were seen by that human!" Draig added with a tone of disappointment.

"I know... but David and his friends all know about us, and they're cool with dragons," Ironstone replied.

"They're the only ones that know about us. Remember what Splinter has taught us, most humans are dangerous, and we have to keep out of their sight.

The humans that are helping us are the exception, you have to remember that!" Draig insisted.

"Okay," Ironstone replied as he held his head low. "I didn't think it was such a big deal."

"No more moonlight hunts either," Esmeralda added with a disapproving snort.

"Really!" Ironstone cried.

"I mean it, you have to lay low from now on," she demanded in an authoritative tone.

A moment later the door to the basement suddenly flew open and David came running down the stairs.

"What did you guys do?" he demanded in loud voice as he glared at them.

"I went outside," Ironstone admitted.

"Well, an Animal Control officer just came to the front door and demanded that I let him in. I told him he couldn't come in until my parents got home, and he said he would be back with a warrant."

"What reason did he give for coming here?" Esmeralda asked.

"He claimed there was a report of a 'giant lizard' in my backyard," David replied angrily.

"I'm so sorry," Ironstone responded in a meek voice.

"I better call Kevin and let him know what's happened," David said as his worst fear had just been realized.

"Kevin, it's me, we have a problem," David said in a frantic tone the second Kevin answered.

"What's wrong?"

"Someone saw Ironstone outside my house and they reported it to animal control. I think they are coming back with a warrant so they can search the house. What should I do? My parents won't be back for several hours," David confessed.

"My dad will be home soon, and I think Emalyn's mom is off work today... let me make a few calls and see what I can arrange," Kevin replied.

"Okay," David said in a nervous tone. After Kevin hung up, he went to the front room and kept a look out for the Animal Control Officer.

Then, after what seemed like a lifetime of waiting, his phone finally rang.

"What took so long?" David asked.

"I'm sorry, I had to coordinate a bunch of things with multiple people. Emalyn and her mom will be over to your house shortly. I want you to get the dragons ready to go on a road trip. Make sure you have enough food and water for a couple of days, and a bunch of blankets to keep them out of sight while we are on the road. My dad will be over shortly to help out too," Kevin assured him.

"Hurry," David pleaded before hanging up. Then he took the dragons up to the garage and grabbed food and water for them.

"What's going on?" Esmeralda asked in a worried tone.

"We're going on a trip," David replied. Then he hugged each Fire Dragon hoping it would comfort them.

The dragons could tell things were not looking good, despite David's attempt to hide the severity of the situation.

"What's going to happen to us?" Esmeralda asked.

"It's time to find you a new home," David replied as he wiped his eyes.

"Is it that lake you and Kevin were talking about last month?" she asked innocently.

"Yes," David replied with a half-hearted smile.

"What if that man comes back looking for us?" Esmeralda asked.

"Don't worry, we are going to be long gone before he comes back," David insisted even though his hopes were fading with each passing minute. When he heard the doorbell ring, he jumped up, and ran to the front door to see who it was. His heart was pounding in his chest as he peered through the peephole, praying it wasn't going to be the Animal Control Officer on the other side of the door.

"Thank goodness it's you," David exclaimed as he rushed Kevin and Emalyn inside.

"Will you open the garage door so my dad and Emalyn's mom can back their vehicles in. We don't want your neighbors seeing what we are doing," Kevin said in a hurried voice.

"Okay," David replied as he rushed back into the garage.

"What's going on?" Draig asked.

"I need you to stay back, Kevin's dad and Emalyn's mom are going to back their vehicles in so no one sees you guys," David ordered.

"Okay," Draig replied as he and the other two dragons moved away from the rising garage door.

Once the vehicles were in, David went back into the house to see what the next part of the plan was.

"Can you to put this old dragon costume on your dog Charlie?" Kevin asked.

"Okay, and then what?" David asked.

"Put him in the basement while Emalyn and I load the dragons into the vehicles," Kevin said with a wink.

"Okay," David smiled, when he realized what Kevin was doing.

A few moments later David returned to find Emalyn's mom parked across the street a few houses down, and Kevin's dad had pulled back out into the driveway.

"David, we're ready to go!" Kevin said as he motioned for him to get into the front seat of the truck.

"Did you call your parents and let them know what's going on? Brian asked, once both of the boys were buckled up.

"I did," David replied. "And they know I'm going with you to release the dragons," he added as he looked over his shoulder at the three blanket-covered lumps sitting quietly on the back seat.

"Okay, let's get going," Brian said as he started the truck, but before he could pull out of the driveway, a Sheriff's car blocked him in.

"Turn off your engine!" the Sheriff ordered over the loudspeaker. Brian reluctantly complied as the Sheriff got out of his patrol car and walked over to the window.

"Keep quiet and let me do the talking," Brian said before he rolled down his window. The boys nodded, but David suddenly felt ill when he saw the Animal Control Officer's van pull up next to his house. Then, as if things couldn't get any worse, the Animal Control officer had a piece of paper in his hand that looked like a search warrant.

"Is this your house?" the Sheriff asked in a gruff voice.

"No," Brian replied.

"Are these your kids?" the Sheriff questioned.

"That's my son and his friend David," Brian replied hesitantly.

"That dark haired boy is the one who refused to let me into the house," the Animal Control Officer yelled loud enough for the Sheriff and the rest of the neighborhood to hear him.

"Please remain in your vehicle for a moment," the Sheriff ordered. Then he walked over to the Animal Control Officer only to return a moment later with the warrant in his hand.

"What's going on?" Brian asked.

"A search warrant has been issued to search this house and the premises," the Sheriff replied.

"For what?" Brian asked innocently.

"For the illegal possession, captivity, or breeding of endangered species," the Sheriff replied.

"So, is that like a ticket or something?" Brian questioned.

"Sir, violations of the Endangered Species Act can carry fines up to $250,000 and two years in prison. In addition, any homes or vehicles used in the commission of the crime are subject to the Asset Forfeiture Act," the Sheriff said as he stared suspiciously at the three lumps in the back seat of Brian's truck. David felt his stomach churning as the Sheriff stood there while the Animal Control Officer went into his house and searched it.

A few minutes later the Animal Control Officer came back out holding Charlie who was still dressed in the dragon costume.

"Wait here," the Sheriff ordered. Then he walked over to see what the Animal Control Officer had found inside the house.

David could see the Sheriff laughing as the Animal Control Officer took the dragon costume off of Charlie. The embarrassed man started pointing at them, waving his hand in an angry fashion.

A few minutes later the Sheriff walked back over to the truck and stared at the back seat for a moment.

"Sir, the warrant allows the search of the house and premises, and since you're parked in the driveway the Animal Control Officer has the right to search your vehicle," the Sheriff announced.

"What if I refuse?" Brian said in a defiant tone.

"I would be forced to arrest you for obstruction, and the kids would be taken into protective custody until a suitable guardian picks them up. Either way, your vehicle is going to be searched," the Sheriff insisted in an authoritative tone.

Brian looked over at the boys sympathetically and then said, "Okay, you can search my truck."

"No!" David cried out. "Don't let them take the dragons away!"

"It will be alright!" Brian said as pulled David out of the truck and held him tight.

A moment later the Animal Control Officer opened the back door to the truck and smirked arrogantly when he saw the blanket covered lumps sitting on the back seat. Then he jerked the blanket off to reveal what was hiding under it.

"What are these?" he gasped.

"They look like dragons!" the Sheriff replied as he burst out in laughter. "… stuffed dragons that is!" he laughed so hard that his handcuffs fell off of his duty belt.

"That's not funny!" the Animal Control Officer replied angrily. "I want them arrested!"

"For what...?" the Sheriff said as he tried to regain his composure. "Dressing up a dog to look like a dragon, or making you look like a fool for believing that dragons are real?"

"That's not fair... a concerned citizen called in a report that they saw a four foot lizard-like creature run into their basement," the Animal Control Officer insisted.

"Yeah, but what they failed to mention was the four foot lizard was really just a dog wearing a costume," the sheriff chuckled.

"They're hiding something, I just know it!" the Animal Control Officer insisted.

"Okay, did you find any exotic animals inside the house, or not?" the Sheriff asked.

"I didn't," the Animal Control Officer conceded in a disappointing tone.

"Then you don't require my services any longer," the Sheriff remarked.

"Are we free to go?" Brian asked.

"Yes sir. Just let me move my patrol car out of the way... and sorry for the inconvenience," he added as he walked away.

The Animal Control Officer carefully inspected Charlie's dog tag, and then begrudgingly handed him back to David without apologizing. Then he went back to his van and sped off.

Once Brian was sure that the Sheriff and Animal Control Officer were gone for good, he started his truck and slowly pulled out of the driveway.

"So, where are the real dragons?" David asked in a concerned tone.

"Emalyn's mom has them, and they're at my house waiting for us," Brian replied.

"Oh, thank goodness," David sighed in relief. Then he picked up one of the stuffed animals and threw it at Kevin. "You could have told me they were safe!"

"Sorry, we were all rushing around, and then the Sheriff arrived, and I was too scared to mention it," Kevin admitted.

Once they got back to Brian's house, David and Emalyn switched out the stuffed dragons for the real ones, while Kevin packed up a few more things for the trip.

"Is everyone ready to go to Lake Powell?" Brian asked after he hitched up the trailer to his truck.

"I think so," Kevin replied after he looked over at David and Emalyn.

"Alright, I'm planning to drive through the night so we don't have to worry about the Fire Dragons being seen along the way,"

"Sounds good dad," Kevin said as they headed out.

Chapter 9

The drive to Lake Powell was long, but it gave everyone time to adjust to the fact that the Fire Dragons would soon be gone. Splinter and Striker did what they could to keep the mood light by poking each other and playing keep away with a ball of string.

Once they turned off the highway and started down a forgotten gravel road, David handed out the last of the dragon treats. He knew letting them go was the right thing to do, but it was still going to be hard to say good-bye.

"This road is pretty rough," Brian said under his breath as he slowed down to keep the trailer from being damaged.

"How much further is it?" Emalyn asked when she noticed a faint glow on the horizon.

"The GPS says 15 miles, but it might take a while to get there depending on how much worse this road gets. Typically, the further you get from the main road, the more the road you're on deteriorates," Brian remarked.

"Okay," Emalyn replied as she held onto the seatbelt to prevent being bounced around.

As they continued down the road, it worsened as predicted, and Brian had to shift into four-wheel drive to continue. "I hope we can get back out," he said when the truck barely made it across a washed out section of the road. After that, they continued on for several more miles until the road abruptly ended at a large flat overlook.

"This must be it," Brian exclaimed. Then after he parked the truck, they all got out and started looking around for the abandoned mine entrance.

"Anyone see anything?" Brian asked as they searched the area several times to no avail.

"There's something over here," Emalyn announced when she noticed a dark opening behind some scrub brush that the rising sun had just illuminated.

"It might be unstable," Brian warned as he peeked inside.

"I'll go check it out," Splinter offered.

"I'll come with you," Esmeralda said as she cautiously followed after her.

"Does it look safe?" Brian asked as waited at the entrance.

"It's fine... we're going to go further back inside," Splinter replied. The main tunnel split into two and the dragons went in separate directions. Each of those tunnels branched off forming a network of interconnecting tunnels. Splinter turned back and then waited for Esmeralda where they had first split up.

"What do think?" Splinter asked when Esmeralda met up with her.

"It's going to take us awhile to figure out where all of these tunnels and shafts go," she replied with a look of excitement.

"I know, you and your brothers will have lots of fun exploring," Splinter replied.

"I hope David is okay with us staying here," Esmeralda said with a sadness in her voice.

"He is going to miss you and your brothers, but he is strong, and he only wants what's best for you."

"I will always remember him, and his friends," Esmeralda admitted.

"I'm sure they will all come back to see you whenever they can," Splinter declared.

"I hope so."

"We should probably head back so the others don't start to worry about us," Splinter suggested.

When David saw Splinter and Esmeralda come out of the mine he ran over and greeted them.

"What's it like inside there?" he asked.

"It's perfect," Esmeralda replied. "There are numerous tunnels and shafts along with several large underground rooms. I think my brothers and I will be very happy here."

"I'm glad to hear that," David replied, sounding a bit mournful.

"You can come visit us as often as you want," Esmeralda said encouragingly.

"I will," David replied as he patted her on the head.

"We're going in for a look," Draig said as he and Ironstone flew into the mine.

A moment later Ironstone came flying back out screaming, "Something attacked me!" as a little brown bat fluttered past him.

"It's just a bat, you big baby," David said as everyone burst out laughing.

"Whew!" Ironstone replied, looking a bit embarrassed. "I thought those things only lived in caves."

"It's actually a good sign. Bats wouldn't be in there unless it had been abandoned for a long time," David replied.

"Hey, come look at this," Kevin said as he pointed southward. "The lake is just below us, so you should be able to swoop down at night and catch all the fish you can eat."

"Ooh, I like the sound of that," Ironstone replied as he peered down at the lake and licked his chops.

"Ironstone will eat anything," Draig jested.

"Except vegetables," Esmeralda added with a snicker.

"No dragon eats vegetables!" Ironstone replied indignantly.

"Neither does my dad," Kevin joked.

"Well he must be part dragon," Draig said with a smile.

"I don't know about that, but after being up all night long, I'm tired. If anyone else wants to join me for a nap, I'll be inside the pop-up," Brian remarked.

"I'm actually pretty worn out. I think I'll go in and get some rest too," Kevin said with a yawn. David and Emalyn followed him in, while the dragons went back to explore more of the mine.

"How long are we going to stay here?" David asked once they were inside.

"After we get some rest, we'll have dinner together, and then it will be time to say good-bye," Brian replied with a hint of sadness in his voice.

"Thanks for helping us," David said as he plopped down on the bed.

"My pleasure," Brian replied.

Later that day, Brian woke up from his nap and saw that the Fire Dragons had come inside and were curled up next to David, while Splinter and Striker were both asleep next to Kevin and Emalyn.

"Awe, everyone has a pet dragon," he muttered under his breath. Then he got out his smart phone and took a picture of everyone sleeping peacefully next to their dragons, before heading outside to start the campfire.

Not long after the fire was burning, Splinter came out and sat down near the package of hotdogs he had taken out of the cooler.

"You can have one," Brian said as he opened the package for her.

"Thanks, you're a good human. I can see where Kevin gets his kind heart. Perhaps one day all humans and dragon will become friends," Splinter said after she gulped the treat down.

"I hope so," Brian said with a smile. Then he gently patted her on the head, and handed her another hotdog.

About the Series

The Dragon Adventure Series was inspired by my son and his room filled with dragon art, books, and posters honoring the beloved creatures. In addition, my family's surname is of Welsh origin, so it seemed fitting to incorporate the Welsh dragon, *Y DDraig Goch* into the storyline. Of course I shortened his name to Draig Goch, and added a host of friends to make the adventure come alive.

The rich mining history and unique geographical locations used in this series are inspired by real events and locations in Colorado, Wales, and Ireland. Some of the location names have been modified to fit the story, but anyone looking at a map should be able to identify their origin.

My hope is that this series will ignite the imagination of young readers and anyone else who loves dragons as much as my family does. If you have any comments or questions, please feel free to contact me at the email address below, and I will make every effort to reply back.

Thanks again,
Ben L. Hughes

Email: kelso1901@yahoo.com

Made in the USA
Middletown, DE
04 October 2015